Vinnie
Takes a Bow

RUTH LERNER PERLE

Illustrated by Richard Max Kolding

Grolier Enterprises, Inc.   Danbury, Connecticut

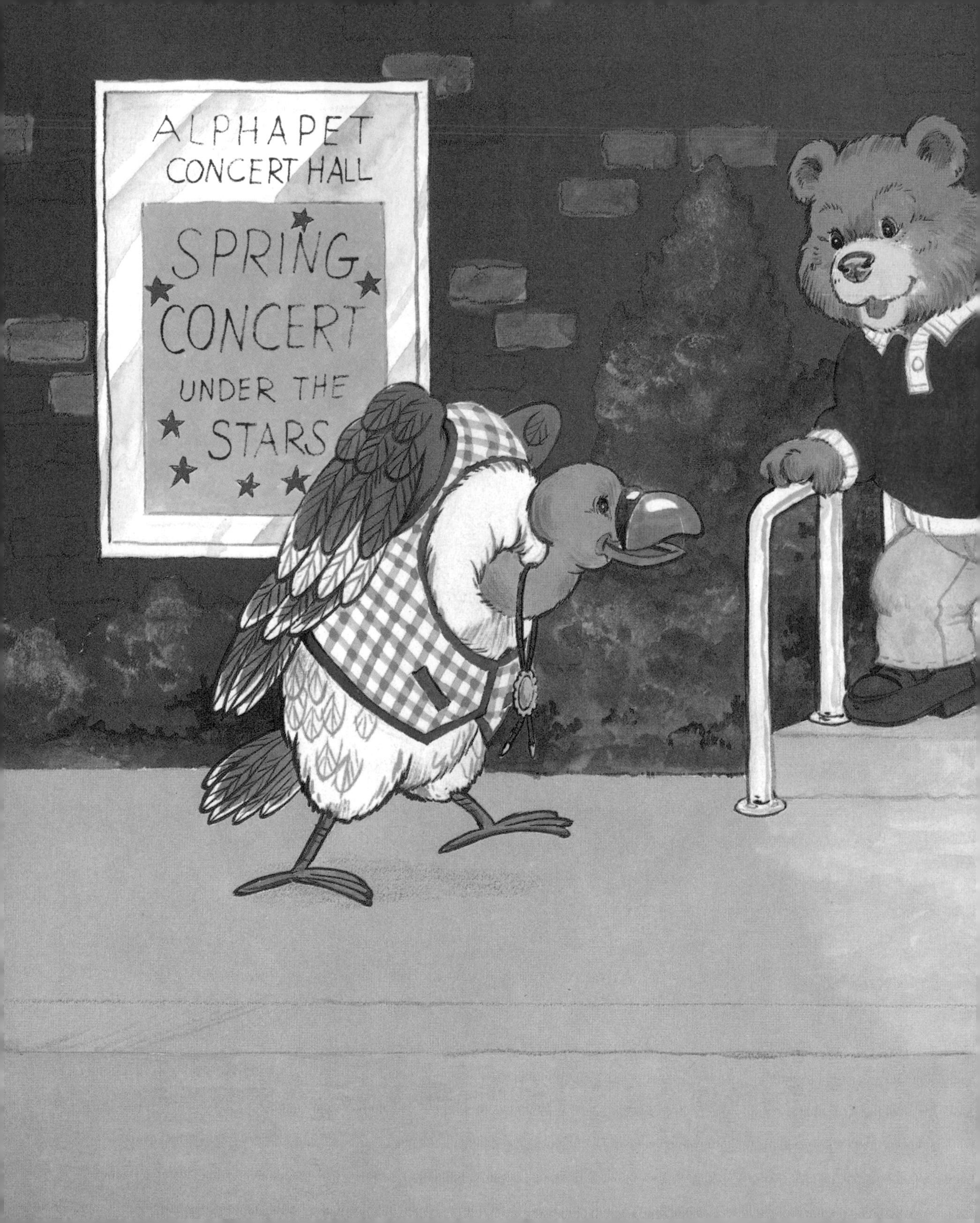
ALPHAPET
CONCERT HALL
SPRING
CONCERT
UNDER THE
STARS

One day, Vinnie the Vocal Vulture was walking down Main Street when he saw some of his friends coming down the steps of the AlphaPet Concert Hall.

"Good morning, Vinnie!" called Bradley the Brave Bear. "You're just the person we're looking for."

"A very, very good morning to you too, my dear Bradley. And why might you all be looking for me, dear friends?" Vinnie asked.

"We're all volunteering to play in the spring concert, and we need someone who can play the violin," said Gertie the Grungy Goat. "We know you are a wonderful violinist, Vinnie. Will you play with us?"

"Play with you? Play with you?" Vinnie said. "Why, it would give me great pleasure, the very greatest of pleasures, to play with you. If I've said it once, I've said it a hundred . . . no, a thousand times. There's nothing as wonderful as playing with friends. I'll play anything you like—football, baseball, jacks, hide-and-seek, marbles. . . ."

"Stop! Stop! You've missed the whole point, Vinnie!" Nelly the Naughty Newt shouted. "Listen! We want you to play your violin in the *orchestra*! We'll be playing outdoors under the stars."

"Yes," added Wendy the Wise Woodchuck. "We're having a rehearsal tomorrow. Bring your violin and meet us here at sundown. Don't forget, tomorrow at sundown!"

"How delightful! Perfectly delightful!" Vinnie said. "I'd love to play my violin under the stars! The twinkling, glistening, shining stars. The bright and beautiful, glittering stars."

The AlphaPets waved good-bye and hurried off, shaking their heads.

"That Vinnie sure can talk!" said Nelly.

"Does he ever stop to listen?" asked Queenie the Quiet Quail.

The next afternoon, Vinnie took out his violin and made sure that it was properly tuned. He tested the bow and the vibrations each string made. That evening, he polished his instrument and placed it in its case.

"I want to be sure that everything goes well at the rehearsal," Vinnie thought. Then he scratched his head and said to himself, "Now, let me see, when *is* that rehearsal? What did Wendy say? Is it Sunday at two? Tomorrow at sunrise? Is it Monday at noon?"

Just then, Gertie and Monty the Mimicking Mouse rang Vinnie's doorbell.

"Why weren't you at rehearsal?" Gertie asked Vinnie as soon as he opened the door. "We waited and waited, but you didn't show up."

"You didn't show up. Why?" Monty said.

"My word!" Vinnie cried. "How could I have missed the rehearsal? How is it possible? Why, I especially prepared my violin. I cleaned it and polished it and tuned it ever so carefully. I truly, truly planned on coming to the rehearsal, but I wasn't sure of the time. I seem to remember that Wendy said something about Sunday at two down under the stars."

"Wendy said 'tomorrow at sundown.' That was *this* evening," Gertie said. "You weren't listening."

"Yes," Monty agreed. "You weren't listening."

"I'm awfully, horribly, terribly sorry," Vinnie said. "Please come in."

"We've stopped by to tell you that we're playing *Swan Lake*," said Gertie. "Practice the violin part, and be at rehearsal Tuesday morning. You can buy the sheet music at the music store."

"Oh yes, yes indeed, I will go to the store first thing in the morning!" Vinnie exclaimed. "How I do love to go to the store. Yes, indeed! Think of all the things there are to buy. A treasure trove of valuables: crystal vases, vacuum cleaners, velvet pants, weather vanes, ivy vines, Venetian blinds, Victorian chairs, Valentines, vitamins and Viennese cakes, velour coats, vicuña vests, vinegar, vanilla creams, and, of course . . . violets, and veils."

"Good glory!" declared Gertie. "All you do is talk. Don't you ever listen?"

"Good glory!" Monty repeated.

"Have no fear!" Vinnie said. "I'll surely be there Tuesday morning. Indeed I will."

Then the three said good night. Gertie and Monty left Vinnie's house, hoping for the best.

The next morning, Vinnie got up bright and early to go shopping. At the music store, Vinnie looked through the music sheets. But suddenly, he wasn't sure of the name of the music he was supposed to get.

"Now let me see," he thought. "What did Gertie say? Which piece are we playing?" He kept looking through stacks and stacks of music, hoping something would look right. Then he saw a familiar title.

"Aha!" Vinnie said. "That's it! *Swanee River.* How I do love that melody."

Vinnie took the music home and practiced from morning to night for the next two days.

"I know this piece by heart," he thought. "The AlphaPets will be so proud of me. So very, very proud. Yes, indeed. How thrilled they will be when they hear the sweet music my violin makes. I can see it all now. The whole orchestra will stand and applaud me, Vinnie. Vinnie the Vibrant Violinist!"

On Tuesday morning, Vinnie played his piece one more time. Then he checked his vest-pocket watch against the wall clock to be sure he wouldn't be late. He packed his violin carefully and went to the concert hall.

The whole orchestra was already there tuning their instruments.

"Greetings, Vinnie! I'm glad you didn't miss *this* rehearsal," said Sylvester the Stubborn Squirrel, who was standing on the conductor's platform.

Vinnie started to answer Sylvester, but Wendy smiled at him and put her finger over her lips. "*Shh*," Wendy whispered, "We're about to begin."

Vinnie unpacked his violin. He took out his music and placed it on the music stand. When everyone was ready, Sylvester tapped his baton and lifted his arms. The whole orchestra started to play.

Vinnie raised his violin to his chin and placed the bow against the strings. But when he played the first few notes, the orchestra stopped. Everyone turned around to look at him.

Rap, rap rap! went Sylvester's baton. "Vinnie! What's that you're playing?" he asked.

"Uh, *Swanee River,* of course," Vinnie said. "Why, this is one of the finest old songs ever written and . . ."

"No, no, no, no!" Sylvester shouted. "Don't you *ever* listen? We're playing *Swan Lake,* NOT *Swanee River!*

Sylvester grabbed a copy of *Swan Lake* off his music stand and handed it to Vinnie. "Now, try to pay attention, please," he said. "Be sure to keep your eyes on me. When I point my baton your way, it will be your turn to play."

Sylvester tapped his baton, and the orchestra started to play again.

Vinnie felt very embarrassed. He turned to Monty and whispered, "I can explain what happened. You see, when I went to the music store, there were stacks and stacks of music sheets, and . . ."

Vinnie was so busy talking that he didn't see Sylvester motion to him.

"Stop! Stop! Stop!" Sylvester shouted. "Vinnie! It was your turn to play, but what were you doing? Talking, talking, talking, talking! That's what!"

Sylvester wiped the perspiration off his forehead and told the orchestra to take a rest. Then he said to Vinnie, "The concert is tomorrow night. If you don't pay attention, I won't let you play in this orchestra."

Tears filled Vinnie's eyes. "I want to play in this orchestra more than anything," he cried. "What went wrong? Why, oh wh..."

"Listen!" Wendy said.

"Listen to what?" Vinnie asked.

"Just listen, Vinnie. Listen to what people have to say. Pay attention to what they want. Then you'll know what to do and say," said Wendy. "*That's* communicating."

Then Wendy said, "I'm sure Sylvester will give you another chance if you promise to play when it's your turn. And I'll help by reminding you. When you see me wink my eye, you'll know it's your turn. That's communicating without any words at all."

"Agreed!" Vinnie said. "My eyes are open. My lips are sealed!" Vinnie pretended to lock his lips and throw away the key.

On the evening of the concert, the members of
the AlphaPet Orchestra were on stage, tuning their
instruments.

"I wonder if Vinnie will get here in time," Queenie
whispered.

"I wonder if he'll bring the right music," Nelly said.

"I wonder if he'll know when it's his turn to play,"
added Herbie.

"I wonder if he'll show up at all!" said Gertie.

"I wonder, too," Monty repeated.

Just then, Vinnie arrived. He smiled at his friends, bowed to the conductor, took out his violin, and was ready to play.

And play he did! He saw Wendy out of the corner of his eye, but he didn't need any help. None at all. When Sylvester signaled him to play, Vinnie's violin sang the sweetest music anyone had ever heard.

When the concert was over, the people in the audience jumped to their feet. "Vinnie! Vinnie!" they called.

Then Vinnie stepped up to the microphone and said, "Ladies and gentlemen, boys and girls, grandmas, grandpas, uncles, aunts, and little babies, I hope you have enjoyed this year's spring concert performance. That's a performance played in *concert*, ladies and gentlemen! Doing things *in concert* means doing things together. Ah, yes! And *how* can people get things done together? I'll tell you how. By communicating. That's right! *Communicating.* Giving and taking, seeing and showing, listening and talking, and, of course . . . making beautiful music together. If I've said it once, I've said it a hundred . . . no, a thousand times. That's right, a *thousand* times! People should stop talking so much and start listening. Yes, indeed! And furthermore . . ."

"Oh, no!" sighed Gertie. "Here we go again!"

"Here we go again!" Monty agreed.

I'll listen while you say these words.

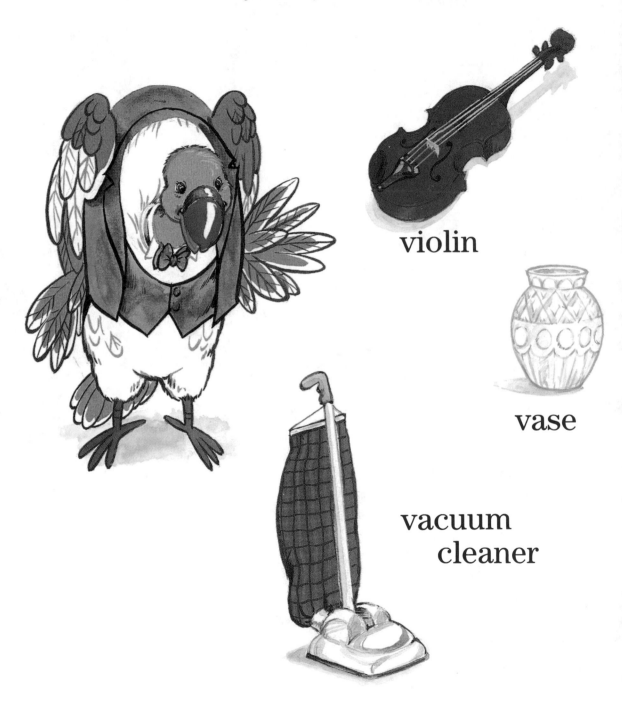

violin

vase

vacuum
cleaner

vest

violets

vegetables

volcano

Look back at the pictures in this book and try to find these and other things that begin with the letter V.

Know Your Alphabet

Aa Bb

Gg Hh

Mm Nn Oo Pp

Uu Vv Ww